Peaceful Magical Dreams

20 Loving Bedtime Stories of Calmness for Young Minds Ages 4-8

Bruce Henry

Table of Contents

Introduction

Peaceful Magical Dreams is a bedtime storybook for children ages 4 to 8 years. It is specially created to bring them the comfort of a peaceful and calm mind, lulled by the magic of loving thoughts, fantasy, and creative characters that take them on adventures in their imagination as they sleep.

Compiled in here are twenty short stories based on the themes of growing up, learning to share, love, be kind, support each other, be helpful, heal others in pain, and many more such positive and noble values which all children will benefit from hearing about.

Each value or lesson is imparted through an adventurous and fun story of mythical beings, believed to be magical, who can be seen only by those with pure hearts. The fact that Tommy, Amiya and Claire, the three protagonists of these stories, can see these creatures is a commentary on the essence of all childhood experiences—an innocence and purity which is often missing once growing up has happened for many children.

The stories are an inspiring reminder to all children to retain their childlike hearts that trust in the power of good—the power that enables light, goodness, safety, protection, love and happiness to prevail.

This ability to retain a childlike innocence throughout life comes only if one believes in magical realities—such is the message of this book, and it is symbolic, rather than literal, ultimately. Once people become adults/aged, being childlike requires believing in childhood itself, a time when the imagination made anything and everything possible, and when there was never a time to feel sad for too long.

Children have a great power which is usually forgotten by adulthood owing to life's endless challenges and the realities of the big, big world out there. If they can be supported in remembering their faithful, magical-seeming ability to be pure, noble, and good, even in the face of obstacles in this modern day and age of corruption and the human state of affairs, they will undoubtedly take the lead in becoming change-makers in our society.

Peaceful Magical Dreams will also give them a way to calm down after any stress they may have experienced during their active and energetic days, which in this era, comes with the stress of screen time experiences, and virtual reality engagements like video games, I-pads, and phones. This book will help remind children that truth is often found in the simplest of all places—out in nature, under the big sky, with green trees around, and a consciousness of Mother Nature whose lap is always ready to nurture us and care for us.

Chapter 1:

Amiya's Toys Come to Life

Once upon a time, in a place called the Snohomish countryside, there lived a young girl called Amiya who loved to play with her toys. Amiya was 5 years old; she had beautiful curly brown hair, and lovely brown eyes that were kind. She was not to be found among elders or adults in her family. Instead, Amiya was mostly found in her garden with the flowers, the beetles, or in her room with her toys.

One afternoon, Amiya was sitting with Teddy, the teddy bear, and her other toys like Barbie, Miss Mermaid, Sophia the Princess, a group of ducklings, and their Momma duckling—all of whom she had put close to herself in a circle on the pink rug in her room.

"Teddy!" she said to the brown little bear made of the softest of furs, "what do you do when I'm not looking?" Amiya kept quiet for a few moments, hoping he would talk.

Her teddy bear had black eyes that seemed to stare back at her, his smile ever the same, reflecting a hint of joy. Teddy gave no response. He was, after all, only a toy, or so thought most people. Amiya, however, always felt like speaking to him—as though it was only natural that he speak to her.

"Teddy," she spoke to him again, holding his curved little hands this time and giving them a gentle squeeze, "can you hear me? I think I saw a big bear one time from my window. He looked a lot like you!"

When she didn't hear a reply from Teddy, she felt a bit sad, and got up and went to her mother.

"Mumma, can you pick me up?" she said to her mother, hugging her and tugging at her clothes. Her mother was busy baking cookies in the kitchen.

Amiya's mother understood that Amiya was sad. "What is it dear? What are you upset about?" she asked her daughter, still busy with the baking.

Tears started flowing out of Amiya's eyes; she started to sob.

"Mumma, Teddy isn't talking to me," she said with tearful eyes, her voice choking.

"Oh sweetie, I'm sorry you're hurt, but you know teddy bears don't talk. They're not like us, Amiya," she replied, holding Amiya now.

These words of her mother's made her cry out now. Amiya simply couldn't accept that her toys didn't talk. She collapsed on the kitchen floor in sorrow.

Just then, Amiya's father returned home from work and came into the kitchen to try and console Amiya. Both her mother and her father tried their best to make her happy again. They showed her a nice cartoon on the television and called up one of her cousins so she could speak to Amiya, but nothing brought Amiya's joy back. She simply wanted her teddy bear to talk to her.

Soon it was evening, and Amiya went to bed earlier than usual as she was exhausted from all the crying. Her mom read her a bedtime story and soon she was fast asleep.

As she was sleeping, a very deeply magical thing started happening. First, Amiya stirred out of her slumber as she felt something soft and light sitting on her blanket, around her tummy. A small night light glowed in the corner of her room. Suddenly, something or someone seemed to be jumping up and down on her tummy!

Amiya, getting up and blinking, rubbed her eyes to try and see what was going on in her room, thinking maybe her mom had come. Instead of her Mumma, she saw only her teddy bear sitting on her blanket.

"Teddy? How did you get here?" she said, speaking softly, more to herself, trailing off with a yawn, almost ready to lay back down, when suddenly she found Teddy speaking back to her.

"Amiya! I went climbing. I can walk!" spoke a gruff teddy bear voice. Not just that, but Teddy, the teddy bear, stood up and came closer to Amiya, holding her hand and giving it a gentle shake as if to say 'Hello.'

Happy all of a sudden by this magical revelation, Amiya laughed out a little giggle, and now, not at all surprised, shook back Teddy's hand.

"How do you do? I knew you could talk, Teddy! I was feeling so sad before," she said.

"Sorry about that, little one. We toys can't talk in front of people. Big people don't understand us," replied Teddy, who then jumped and settled himself on Amiya's shoulder.

"Teddy, you're alive... this is fun...," laughed Amiya, holding him momentarily so he wouldn't fall off.

"Amiya, come with me and the others to the garden. We have something to share with you!" said Teddy, much to Amiya's surprise.

"The others?" she asked, getting up and out of bed, eager to find out where this new adventure would lead.

Instantly she found all her toys starting to get up from their places and move across the floor to the door, waving at Amiya as they went by.

"Teddy! This is amazing!" she whispered, "My toys can walk and talk! Wow!"

And hushing then, she followed her toys, with Teddy on her shoulder, out the front door, and into their lush green garden. There, by a big tree which always had little golden electric lights blinking at night, she and all her toys sat down in a circle.

Teddy spoke first:

"Let's introduce ourselves by saying something nice!"

"Okay," replied Amiya, fascinated; she went first.

"Miss Mermaid, I've always liked your blue ocean dress. And Barbie, I like that your hair always smells so nice," Amiya said, so happy that she could express herself.

"Oh, thank you; blue is the only color I know that makes me feel fulfilled," replied little Miss Mermaid.

"My hair smells nice? I didn't know!" exclaimed Barbie.

The introductions went on for some time.

After that, Miss Mermaid said, "We are here to share with you, Amiya, now that you know us, that there's a whole world of Nature beings in our very own Snohomish region; they aren't found everywhere, but they're definitely there in the mountains, and the ocean nearby."

"Really?" asked Amiya, curious. "When do I get to see them?"

"When you start looking! Be ready to go on adventures with your friends Claire and Tommy! You three will find the fairy folk, the gnomes, the dwarves and the elves, all hidden in this realm. If you believe in magic, they will start appearing!" said Teddy.

Amiya inhaled, getting a great feeling about all this. Her mind began to wonder about and imagine the kinds of beings out there and what they could do.

"I'm so happy; I'm never going to feel alone now. We can have so much fun now!" she said to her lovely toys who were just as excited as her.

"Yes, Amiya. Fun is exactly it! But lessons too—you'll see. And remember, don't tell the parents about us!" said Teddy.

Amiya promised them she wouldn't tell any of the adults, and she and the toys all returned to their room quietly without waking her parents. Teddy entered last and made sure that the front door was locked behind them after they all came in.

"And so, it begins..." he whispered before settling into his little bed in the toy's corner. All the toys peacefully asleep now, Amiya dreamt of fairylands and beings who in every age made themselves known to children with pure hearts.

Chapter 2:

Claire Discovers a Fairy House

Little Amiya had two very good friends in the neighborhood—6-year-old Claire, and 8-year-old Tommy. In the morning after a very fun night with her toys, Amiya had to go to school, but when she returned, she decided to tell her best friends about her grand discovery of the previous night.

"Claire! Are you coming over today?" Amiya said on the phone to Claire, a girl whose beautiful golden hair often fell all over her fair face and blue eyes when she tumbled around to play.

"I have something really fun to tell you!" Amiya said to her in a whisper full of excitement.

Claire, getting really curious, answered her, "What is it? Can you tell me on the phone?"

"No, I can't tell you right now... Come to my house today," answered Amiya.

"Okay, Tommy and I are going to come and see you," replied Claire, who then called up Tommy and planned to go and see their friend Amiya.

Claire loved to sing. On the way to Amiya's house, walking with Tommy, she began to sing a song that she had created on her own recently.

"All the world can be my friend...... La La La-La, La La-La..... "

Laughing and hopping in her pink frock, skipping every now and then, Claire entered Amiya's front garden along with Tommy, who made sure they latched the gate behind them. Up the porch steps and at the front door in a jiffy—they giggled excitedly after pressing the bell.

Amiya opened the door, joyful and smiling. "Hi Tommy, hi Claire... come on in," she said, and stepped aside to let her friends in. Once in Amiya's room, they closed the door, and for a few minutes ran around the room, jumped on the bed, and had a few falls here and there.

Finally, Claire sat down in the toys corner and said to Amiya, "Are you going to tell us now?"

Tommy instinctively came down from the bed, and they all sat together on the floor rug on their knees.

"It's my toys! I have to tell you... it's a secret. Promise me you won't tell anybody," Spoke Amiya, a bit softly, but with seriousness.

Claire and Tommy looked at each other and smiled mischievously. They promised.

Having a peaceful sparkle in her eyes then, Amiya picked up her Barbie doll and teddy bear and brought them close to her, hugging them to her body.

"My toys can talk," she said, bending over to give them a full and complete hug.

"Really?" said Claire. "Can you make them say something?"

"Umm.... they don't talk in front of others. We had a secret meeting last night by the big tree in my garden! They're just like us!"

Looking wild with excitement now, Tommy and Claire picked up a few of her toys and tried saying different things, still trying to fathom what it would be like to actually hear them talk back.

"What did they say to you, Amiya?" said Tommy suddenly.

"They said that there's Nature beings and fairies... and gnomes and dwarves here in Snohomish.... isn't that fun?!" she replied, excitedly.

"What?! Real fairies? No kidding!" cried Tommy.

"I want to meet them!" said Claire, looking at Tommy.

Just then Amiya's mother came looking for them; her footsteps could be heard in the hallway outside the room.

"We could go look for them tonight! You can come over to my house! Maybe my garden has secret fairy hideout spots!" said Tommy, ideas running through his head about searching for these fairies.

The door swung open just then, and Amiya's mother popped in the room.

"Children, I have treats in the kitchen for you all. But no one's going anywhere in the night looking for fairies! Okay? It's not safe. Now come along..., " she said, and walked back to the kitchen, leaving the door open.

The children giggled amongst themselves; the joy in their hearts was of another world. They knew this was too good to let go—fairies and a world full of magical creatures coming to life?! They decided they would do something, even if it wasn't going anywhere in the night.

While walking back later to their homes, Claire and Tommy saw some of the other neighborhood children playing. Claire decided she was going to play with them.

So, Tommy went back home, while Claire tried to play with the circle of children who, it turned out didn't welcome her.

Claire felt hurt inside. Standing there, for a moment, she felt she was about to cry, when suddenly, Ms. Anita, who lived down the street, approached them. She had seen what had happened. Coming close, she put a gentle hand on Claire's shoulder, bent down, and whispered something to her to make her feel better.

"Claire, I'm Anita. Don't feel bad about this. These children are missing out on the real fun. I want to show you something. Will you come with me?" she whispered. Claire looked up; a few tears had rolled down from her eyes.

"I have a fairy house in my garden...," said Anita, her hazel eyes twinkling with charm, wonder and kindness.

That brought a smile to Claire, and it was decided—they walked together, hand in hand, to Anita's home and garden; the house itself was a very pretty, small and snug, pink and greenhouse. Claire became enchanted by the very sight of it. And then, walking on the garden grass, they came to the promised fairy house—it was under a big silver fir tree.

The fairy house was so lovely to behold—a little wooden house, with windows the size of fingernails, and a door the size of a thumb. Neat little fairy lamps were lit around the fairy house in a tiny garden made with seashells, mud, and a bit of grass. Small mushrooms were present too, all of different colors, some having white spots on them, and there was little confetti strewn around in the fairy garden, giving it the appearance of having tiny shiny sea pearls spread all over. It was a pretty sight to behold—one teeming with life it seemed!

Claire now began to wonder what would happen if she opened the door to the fairy house. It seemed to be calling to her silently! There was a very tiny bell on the door which she yearned to ring.

However, just then, Anita came back from within the house.

"Little one, it's getting dark... you should probably run along now," said Anita, and it was time to go home. Claire decided she would come back again and try to bring Tommy and Amiya next time.

The next day Claire told Tommy and Amiya about her discovery at Anita's house, and the kind words Anita spoke to her. They were thrilled.

"Will she be nice to us too?" asked Amiya, who wasn't always confident around adults.

"Yeah, I think so..." responded Claire, sounding very thoughtful and serious.

"Let's go tomorrow," Claire proposed. And the other two agreed.

That night, Claire, Amiya and Tommy all started spinning their imaginations with dreams of fairies, elves, dwarves, and other creatures that were beautiful and magical, of whom they had only heard about. These began to seem just within their reach now. Their adventure was to begin at Anita's house.

Chapter 3:

Claire and Friends Explore Anita's

Little House

Tommy, Claire and Amiya walked over to Anita's home the next afternoon and rang the doorbell.

Tommy, the one who was used to caring for younger siblings, made sure that Amiya and Claire were ready to be at their best behavior before Ms. Anita answered the doorbell.

"Just remember, we need to make her our friend. Let's be the best we've ever been!" he said in low tones, making it sound like a secret mission.

Amiya instantly was reminded of a question she had earlier, and began to say it aloud, "Well, what if the fairy house...."

She was cut off by the door suddenly swinging open, and Anita, the sweet lady with a dear heart as kind as the flowers, was now standing in front of them.

Tommy and Amiya both were stunned for a moment, and just stared at her open-mouthed.

"Oh hello! Who have we here? Claire, I see you brought your friends along! How lovely! Come in please," said Anita and made way for them to enter a most beautifully lit home with lamps of all shapes and sizes, beautiful white furniture that was simple and clean, a lot of paintings of farms and maidens hanging on walls, and pretty clay pottery placed in many nooks around the house.

"What are your names?" asked Anita, ushering them toward the pretty and comfortable couches.

"I'm Tommy, and this is Amiya..." replied Tommy, sitting comfortably now. All the children sat excitedly, wondering if Anita was going to tell them stories.

"Those are wonderful names. Would you three like a little tea party?" Anita asked suddenly.

The children looked at each other and grinned. Anita got her answer in their smiles.

In a few minutes, a cute little teapot with teacups and mint tea arrived for them all along with some jaggery cookies. The children and Anita spent some time enjoying the treats and their cozy little tea party. Claire felt happier and happier, inside. She felt at last she had found a friend who was part of a world that was magical already, even though she hadn't actually seen a fairy yet.

"In this world, I have seen many things over the years, children, but rarely have I seen children like yourselves who are so well-behaved, attentive, and curious!" said Anita, at one point.

Amiya, Tommy, and Claire looked at each other and smiled again, satisfied this time that they had done well so far.

"I think all children have a magical purity about them. And if they are sensitive enough, like you all are, they can even look into the deeper hidden things of this universe," Anita added, her voice becoming a whisper toward the end. The silence that followed got the children thinking.

After some more discussion, and finishing their tea and cookies, Tommy requested if they could go and see the fairy house in Anita's garden. Anita, who had alighted their curiosity with stories of fairies and gnomes by now, wholeheartedly agreed to the idea.

Tommy and Amiya, hence, left for the garden. Claire, however, wanted to stay inside. Anita found her something useful to do; she came up with a little cleaning task.

Out in the garden, Tommy and Amiya made their way with awe and wonder to the silver fir tree housing the fairy house at the base of its trunk.

"Ready?" whispered Amiya as she put one hand on the door of the fairy house, ready to open it.

Tommy, holding his breath, replied, "Ready!"

Just as Amiya was about to open it, a little winged creature whizzed past them really fast, spreading a dazzling dust as it went by.

"Woah! Did you see that Amiya?" squawked Tommy. Shaking his head and clearing the dust away from his nose; it almost made him sneeze. He looked around now.

"Yeah! I saw! I think it's the fairies!... They're here.... Tommy!" Amiya replied, looking around frantically now, wondering where the fairy went.

In the meanwhile, Claire had gone to one of the rooms in the house that needed cleaning. It was a room with a lot of books and bundles of newspapers. She had a cleaning cloth in her hand and got to work by picking one book at a time and wiping it clean with the wet cloth in her hand.

Suddenly, as she sat there on the floor, cleaning away the fifth book, a little creature appeared out of nowhere, and toppled the whole pile of books that was next to her!

"Uhh... who's there? What's going on?" stuttered Claire, staring in a befuddled way into the dimly lit space. The little creature had vanished.

Appearing another time, in bright, yellow-colored clothes, the little creature was about to topple another pile of dusty books, on to Claire this time. Claire, however, overcame her bewilderment at seeing a real Nature being for the first time and showed sympathy on this little mischief maker. She addressed him in a sweet sing-song way.

"You know that's not a good thing to do," she said, quite politely.

The little being froze for a moment, and, shaking his head, peered at her from behind the books. His pointy ears were clearly in view.

"No, it's not," came his squeaky voice. After that, he came out fully into view. Giving up his game, he sat down cross-legged on the rug, and started to cry.

Claire was astonished. She felt sorry for him.

"Oh, you poor dear! Whatever's making you cry?" asked Claire, her heart melting now. She crouched down, not minding getting dirty, and moved closer so she could speak to this little guest who had arrived out of nowhere. He was only the size of her hand. He kept crying for a while, after which he became okay and told Claire his name. And she told him her name.

The grandfather clock struck 6 o'clock just then, and the children heard it clearly. It was time to head home soon. Claire said a hurried goodbye to the gnome and came running out of the dusty room. Tommy and Amiya also came running back inside from the garden. As soon as they all met, they began spilling out their stories of meeting the beautiful fairy in the garden and the little gnome in the dusty room.

Sparkles of joy and excitement beamed from their faces as they stood in the living room blurting out their discoveries.

"What was the gnome's name, Claire?" asked Tommy, who had never seen a gnome in his life.

"Mucklebuckle, he told me. It's a funny name, isn't it?" replied Claire, while Anita, who was in the kitchen, packed them a few treats for their way back home.

"What about the fairy? What is her name?" asked Claire now, with equal fascination in her eyes, never having met a fairy.

"Her name is Loopy Iris," answered Amiya, happily.

"Awww! I want to see her too!" sighed Claire.

Just then, Anita handed them banana bread slices wrapped up in foil to take back home. It was time to go then and come back another time.

"Thank you so much, Anita. We really enjoyed ourselves," said Tommy on behalf of all of them. Off they went then, back home, with the freshest hope for what magical wonders lay waiting for them in the coming days ahead.

Chapter 4:

Mucklebuckle and Loopy Iris

After a couple of days, on a fine afternoon, the children gathered at Claire's home to bake cookies together with Claire's mother. When the cookies were ready, they packed some in a basket for Anita, putting some thought into their presentation as well.

"I'll be the one to knock on the door since I'm the eldest," said Tommy without any hesitation.

"Can I give her the basket?" asked Amiya.

"Okay, but what about me? What will I do?" asked Claire.

"Maybe you can be the first one to greet Anita when she opens the door!" answered Tommy.

And in this way, they all had something to do. Along they went that afternoon and reached Anita's door once again at the sweet little pink and green house down the street. The sky was peaceful and cloudy, and the birds were sweetly chirping away in her garden; Anita herself was very cheerful; she seemed to be humming a tune when she opened the door.

"Oh, it's you all again! How lovely! Come in!" said the gracious and kind Anita.

"And what is this? Is it for me?" she asked, finding Amiya handing her the basket.

"We made some cookies for you," said Amiya with such fondness that Anita bent down and gave them all a warm hug.

"Would you like to go out and play in the garden again today?" Anita asked them.

"Oh yes! We were just about to ask you that," came Tommy's reply and, looking at Amiya with excitement, Tommy decided to wait no more. He and Amiya sped off to the garden to find the little fairy house.

Claire, however, stayed back and decided to tell Anita about the little gnome, Mucklebuckle, whom she had met a few days ago.

"Interesting... you say he's a gnome?" said Anita with a lot of thought and curiosity.

"Yes..." said Claire, clasping her hands joyfully.

"Why don't you try cleaning some more today, and if he comes again, talk to him? Maybe try finding out what he's after? Or what's making him sad?" suggested Anita.

"Okay," said Claire, and went immediately to find the cleaning supplies.

While Claire went about looking for Mucklebuckle, the other two children—Tommy and Amiya—were busy searching for Loopy Iris, the pretty fairy they had seen last time fluttering about in the flowers. The two of them went down on their knees, and crawled all around the flower beds, looking for the fairy who had only stopped to introduce herself last time.

"Loopy Iris! Loopy Iris!" called out Amiya loudly, again and again; she looked up every now and then in case Loopy Iris was flying above the tops of the flowers. And sure enough! They soon spotted her in the corner of the garden flying above some pink-colored flowers. They went over to her.

As they approached, Loopy Iris stopped hovering and landed over one of the flowers.

"Lovely children," she said, "How nice you came again!"

Tommy and Amiya settled on the ground close to her.

"Hi," they replied to the fairy.

"I feel you both bring happiness," said Loopy Iris. "Hence, I will share a secret to more happiness with you children."

And she went on to tell them about how to call for help and protection if they are ever in a situation which is scary.

"Does that mean we can call out whenever we like?" asked Amiya.

"Yes, Amiya. You see, your mind is like an antenna—you can send any message or call for help using your mind power... the angels are always listening, and they will come rushing to help you when you need extra help," she continued, pointing her tiny fingers to her little head.

Tommy was deep in thought. After a moment, he ventured to ask a question.

"What if an angel sends us a message back to tell us what to do? I mean, what if they don't come all the way, but just try to say something back? Will we hear them? If they speak?" he asked curiously.

"Tommy, that is a good question. If an angel tries to speak to you, then you need to 'listen with your heart'. You have a very helpful heart which is like the receiving set of a radio. You can always find your answer by tuning your heart radio and listening for the answer," she replied.

Understanding things better now, Tommy asked another question:

"Have you always lived here, Loopy Iris?"

"Me? Oh yes! Ever since I was born," she replied, shining light and scattering dust now as she flew to nearby flowers.

Back in the house, Claire had found Mucklebuckle toppling around books again, looking sad, as if he had given up on life.

"Mucklebuckle, what is it that you're after?" asked Claire, picking up the piles of books he had just toppled.

Feeling better because of the sympathy he got, the little gnome stopped his mischief, and sat down like the other day.

"If you really want to know, then hear. I've been given the job of cleaning dusty places. But how I hate dust...." his voice choked up in the middle of his sentence, and he started crying.

"It's okay, don't cry little gnome; I understand," assured Claire. The gnome wiped away tears and continued.

"All this dust—I'm supposed to clean it away so that humans like Anita can be helped secretly. She doesn't have any family living here, you see? I was sent to help her. I'd rather be helping with something better like adventures with the elves to find food for them in the woods, but I have to pass through this stage, and I feel I'll never get past this one," he said, now holding back the tears, and wringing his hands.

"Oh don't worry; what if I help you? You could do this job faster, and then you can go to the woods soon!" replied Claire with a special enthusiasm to help out the gnome.

Feeling completely odd that someone offered him help for the first time in his life, he looked up with eyes full of a new ray of hope; his face then turned into a smile, as though the sunshine had just come out after a dark and rainy day. He got up and did a celebratory dance around Claire.

"Thank you! Oh, thank you!" He sang, and Claire started laughing at his joyful little gesture.

The day ended with the three happy children returning home, discussing what amazing things had happened that day. Claire especially shared how she had helped Mucklebuckle clean the dusty room.

"Every day should be this fun!" said Tommy, and the other two wholeheartedly agreed.

Chapter 5:

A Special Meeting at Wallace

Waterfall

All was peaceful in Snohomish as always. One night, sleeping peacefully in his bed, was Tommy, snoring away. Suddenly he jerked, and there was not a sound more to be heard. Tommy was now having a dream.

He dreamed of a waterfall, and it felt special to him. The water came down and made radiant crystal pools of silvery white foam, turning into magical shiny lights, the water seemed to be alive with magical life under the surface. Tommy thought to himself while dreaming that he had to explore more. So, in the dream, he jumped into the little pool of water, and found his whole-body shimmering now with the same light, little fish moving about close to him with a light of their own. He enjoyed watching the amazing play of lights, water, and the strange radiance when, suddenly, it was all gone, and Tommy found himself in his bed, feeling the thrill of the experience still.

"That was so real!" Tommy whispered to himself. "I must find out where this waterfall is! It must be in Snohomish, and I have to go there!"

In the morning, he called up his friends and told them about the dream. Claire and Amiya were amazed, but Claire was a little doubtful about how they were going to find the waterfall.

"There are so many waterfalls in Snohomish, Tommy. Don't you know?" she said to him, waving her hands in the air, which only her mother, sitting close by, could see.

"Yes, I know Claire. But maybe Anita will know which waterfall was in my dream!" he said with the faith of someone who knew that his true wishes would come true.

He soon called up Anita, and sure enough—Anita knew just the waterfall!

"It seems to me it could be the Wallace Waterfall, Tommy. By the way you describe it, it reminds me of the Wallace Waterfall," she said to him, pleased about hearing of this special dream.

"Can you take us there, Anita?" asked Tommy with hope.

"Ha ha ha, yes! Why not? Let's all make a plan. This would be fun for me. I haven't gone out hiking lately and I've been wanting to. I'd be happy to go with you children," she replied, ready for an adventure.

And so, it was decided.

The next day, being a Sunday, Claire, Tommy, Amiya and Anita all got ready and went for a hike to Wallace Waterfall, which was nearby. It was a lot of walking, but they took breaks in between. At one spot on the trail, they saw a board which read:

Come Forth into the Light of Things, Let Nature be your Teacher. —W. Wordsworth

Full of joy at this special message, which hinted at Tommy's dream, they were even more eager to get to the waterfall now.

Finally, after a while, they reached the waterfall.

It was a sight to behold. Tommy fell in love with the waterfall the moment it came into full view. They were now right next to the falls on some rugged rocks.

No one else was there. Anita advised the children to sit and become quiet so they could feel the stillness behind the rush of the water.

The children understood and sat down close to the water; droplets and sprinkles splashed onto their legs every now and then. It was a refreshing experience.

All three of them closed their eyes, and Anita too sat down and entered the beautiful stillness where all she focused on was the sound of the rushing water. *So powerful!* she thought.

Within the next few minutes, a small bird fluttered by—it was a hummingbird. It hovered here and there, and at one moment, she hovered right in front of the children, her wings flapping fast, making a whizzing and buzzing sound. The children just had to open their eyes to admire how pretty she was in her colors and how fast she was, even friendly.

The hummingbird flew now to the waterfall, as if bringing the children's attention to something there.

And in a moment, the white water seemed to be separating out, a figment leaving the mainstream of rushing water, gliding toward them. It was a spirit—a beautiful silvery white light that looked like a woman, a beautiful lady with silvery white hair, a long robe and an ancient-looking musical instrument in her hands.

"I'm seeing a beautiful ghost," said Claire, as she turned to Anita, but she realized they were seeing the spirit too.

"We are all seeing it, Claire," said Anita, her eyes half open and half closed, smiling peacefully. The spirit came closer, playing a melody of a sweet song as she flew slowly toward them.

"Greetings children," she said, her voice sounding like comforting music.

Tommy stood up and reached out his hand to touch her. He knew he came for a reason there that day, but never had he imagined such a beautiful magical reality which he now saw.

"Who are you? What is your name?" he said, his fingers still reaching out into the space in front of him.

"My name is Serena. You won't be able to touch me, Tommy. I am only a spirit," said the fairy, gliding about, smiling with a secretive smile.

"Oh," said Tommy, and by now the others were standing too.

"You know our names! Are you a fairy? And do you live in the waterfall?" asked Amiya.

"Yes, Amiya. I'm a fairy; some call me the queen fairy. I live here in Wallace Waterfall—it is my abode," replied Serena.

The children, Anita, and Serena began to talk of many things, but most of all, about magic and Nature. Serena told them about how they were meant to come that day—it was destined to happen. Tommy felt pretty cheerful and proud when he heard that.

"I told you both! I knew it had to be! I was right..." he said to them excitedly.

"Children, keep believing in magic—it is only then that you will be able to see more of my kingdom—the elves, the gnomes, the fairies, the dwarves, the animals, the angels and the ascended," she explained. "All of them can teach you important lessons about life, even if they themselves are learning."

"You mean like the gnomes?" asked Claire.

"Yes, Claire, like the gnomes. You are a smart little girl," she added.

"It's about time we start heading back," said Anita now, very politely; she was keeping a track of the time and the amount of daylight. The children, unwilling to leave, said a heartfelt goodbye, still mesmerized and hooked to the picture of Serena till she finally disappeared back into the waterfall.

When they started walking back in silence, Tommy took one last look back at the waterfall behind them. He noticed something.

"Who is that?" he asked, stopping and pointing to a place close to the waterfall.

They all stopped and looked, and saw that on the other side of the river sat a very handsome, tall, and youthful-looking elf with long, pointy ears.

"I think Serena has an admirer..." said Anita, calmly smiling, beginning to walk again. The children looked at each other and shrugged; they continued behind Anita.

And so the journey of the three children began, more fully now, into the hidden world of nature and magic—a journey they embarked on for understanding the very essence of life itself.

Chapter 6:

Tricked by Villio, the Screen

Gnome

It was Tuesday afternoon when Anita called up Claire to let her know that she was a bit under the weather.

"Claire, I won't be able to have you and the others over for a get-together today. I'm sorry about that. Hopefully, I'll get better in a day or two. How about we meet after that?" said Anita.

"Okay. I'm sorry you're not well. Can I get you anything?" said Claire thoughtfully, who had learned a few good things about how to treat elders from her mother.

"Oh, I think I have everything; thanks for asking, Claire. I'll talk to you soon," replied Anita and hung up the phone.

After some time, when Claire met Tommy and Amiya, they wondered what they could do that day. Tommy came up with an idea.

"I know!" he spoke up with enthusiasm, "Let's play video games at my house! My cousin gave me a new video game set last week, and it's really cool! We can even have all three of us playing at the same time!"

"Okay!" replied Claire and Amiya in unison, and off they went, running to Tommy's house.

There they sat in the living room and put on a video game while Tommy's dad was away at work and his mom was busy cleaning in the attic on the uppermost floor of the house. His younger siblings were away at a neighbor's home since their mom needed to work by herself.

Tommy, Amiya, and Claire played and played, and played... Hooked like bees to a beehive, they kept playing the video game for 1 hour, then 2 hours, then 3 hours, till suddenly, out of nowhere, a gnome, dressed in red, appeared.

He hopped and bounced around and spoke to them as he went.

"Hi, I'm Villio! And you must be the children!"

Before any of them had time to respond, Villio opened a little bag and sprinkled around magic dust that flew to all three of them, making them sneeze a couple of times.

"Villio! We don't like this!" said Tommy, after continuing to rub his nose and eyes, trying to clear away the irritation.

Sobs could be heard now, and it was Amiya—she was now silently sobbing as if touched by sadness. Claire and Tommy also started to feel sad now, strangely disgusted as well.

In a minute, all three of them were crying and sobbing.

Villio calmed down and came to a rest on the center table.

"Sorry kids, I'm just doing my job. I'm the screen gnome and this is what I do. Goodbye!" he said, and off he went magically into the thin air from where he'd come—he disappeared!

Claire heard his words, and a strange wise thought struck her like lightning.

"Amiya, Tommy," she said, calming herself now, and wiping away her tears with her wet hands, "we've been tricked by Villio."

"I know why we're feeling sad," she continued.

"Why are we feeling sad, Claire?" asked Amiya, moaning.

"It's because we had too much screen time. We shouldn't be watching too much TV or playing video games for this long," she said emphatically, getting up from the couch now. She went and opened a window.

"Here's some fresh air," she said, as the gentle breeze came in now and brought peace.

Tommy got up, thinking about this, and turned off the video game.

Amiya too stopped sobbing and came to where Claire was standing by the window.

"Do you think other children also feel sad like us when they play too many video games?" asked Amiya, out of curiosity.

"I think so," said Claire, looking out into the nature and trees outside. A few birds were flying around from tree to tree. Greenery was everywhere.

"I think that other children can't see Villio, but he must be coming to them, too, secretly. Villio wants all children to learn their lessons," said Claire.

"When our parents turn off the screens, we cry and we put on a temper tantrum, because we've had so much, and we want to keep going... you know? And we don't want to take their 'no' for an answer," said Claire to both Amiya and Tommy.

"Yeah," replied Tommy, shifting his feet around, "I know that happens. It's happened with me before."

"Okay," said Amiya, with some understanding. "I think I understand— I'm not going to watch too much again."

"Yeah, me neither," said Tommy.

"And I feel the same way," said Claire right after Tommy.

Suddenly, Tommy's mother came down from the attic, and saw the children by the window.

"Oh honey! Your friends are here! How lovely? What are you all going to do? Want to play video games for some time?" she asked, thinking about possible things that may be fun for the children.

"Nooooooooooooooo!" cried all three of them, as though thunderstruck.

Tommy's mom was taken aback by their united "No"; it was as if they were struck by an earthquake or something.

"Okay! Okay! Hmmm... what a strange aversion you all have to that idea!" she commented and went into the kitchen.

"Let's go out and play hide-n-seek in the garden instead!" said Tommy.

"You got it!" said Claire. And off they went without looking back again at the scene of their battle with Villio; they went and played with Mother Nature in the brightness of her sunlight and fresh air amidst the secret hideout spots in Tommy's green and grassy garden.

Chapter 7:

Roll Mine the Naughty Comes to

the Rescue

It was Wednesday, and the sky was filled with grey clouds in the Snohomish Mountains. The children all looked out of their windows with hope; they didn't like getting wet, but today Claire called up Tommy and Amiya and suggested that they go out and play anyway, even if it rained.

"But what if we catch a cold, Claire?" asked Amiya, who, being the youngest, was also fussed about the most by the adults. She was usually told not to play outside when it rained so that she wouldn't catch a cold.

"I know, but we have to take a chance. It's one of those things," said Claire with a very proper and serious tone. She felt she had made her point.

"One of which things?" asked Amiya, not understanding her older friend.

"Umm.... you know, the thing where you do something because it's right and not because it's totally safe?" clarified Claire.

"Uhuh... hmm... okay. I'll really have to get after my mom to let me play out today. And look! It's actually drizzling now!" said Amiya, sounding a bit worried.

"Don't worry, just tell her we're going to brave it. Keep your raincoat ready, Amiya. I'm coming," replied Claire, before heading off to Tommy's house so she could take him along.

At Amiya's house, the three children finally made it to her backyard garden, dressed in brightly colored raincoats and rain boots. Amiya's garden was adjoining the nearby forest. A short walk across the backside of the garden and trees revealed a little creek coming all the way from the heart of the mountains.

"Let's build a walking path across this creek!" said Tommy, who began climbing little rocks and stones to get to the other side.

"Okay!" said Claire and Amiya, and the three children began gathering whatever they could find in nature to create a little walking path that would serve as a path across the creek.

It was pretty slippery with the drizzling, but the children felt like they were on a mission.

"This is fun!" said Amiya, who had now begun to enjoy being outside in the rain.

Just then, however, something unexpected happened.

Tommy slipped while he was carrying a big piece of a wooden tree branch and fell on some rocks. Instantly, he scraped his knee and saw that it began to bleed. Seeing the sight of blood, and feeling the pain, he started to cry. Poor Tommy, he just sat there in the little creek, crying and crying his heart out.

Amiya and Claire felt sorry for him and didn't know what to do. They walked over to him, carefully, so they wouldn't slip like him, and tried to console him. Tommy's cries grew louder and louder, however. Amiya felt so sympathetic, that she too began to weep. Claire was left to her own devices; she walked about restlessly, not knowing what to do now that both were upset.

Just then, out of thin air, appeared a little mountain dwarf dressed in a miner's clothes. He had a pointy hat, rough hands, a little stout body, and a face that revealed blue eyes, a round nose, and a thick beard—Claire was dumbstruck as the dwarf put down his little axe from his shoulders, and said, "Hello!"

She was just about to scream out loud out of fright when suddenly the dwarf extended his hand out and showed her what he had in his hands—shiny gems that looked like diamonds. Amiya and Tommy meanwhile hadn't realized someone had come.

Claire's motivation to cry suddenly went away.

"Who're you, Mister?" she asked politely.

And Tommy looked up for the first time. It was then he realized that a Nature being had joined them.

"I'm good old Roll Mine the Naughty, lads! I'm a dwarf from yon mountain ranges, just off on that side of the hill," said he, pointing to the range of hills toward the East, bowing slightly. "Just extracted some of these rare and precious ones! Like 'em don't you?"

Tommy kept feeling sorry for himself and kept sobbing and sobbing. Amiya, however, was quiet now. She became full of awe for this rare Natural being.

Open-mouthed and wonderstruck, she and Claire kept staring at the dwarf as if they needed someone to shake them out of their fascination.

"Now now, Tommy, you're Tommy, am I right?" asked Roll Mine, turning to Tommy.

"Yeah..." moaned Tommy.

"Tommy, son, that must be hurting. Here, let me see it," he said, and bent down to look at Tommy's knee.

Little bits of curiosity began to replace Tommy's sadness.

"Oh, this is something, yes... quite something... I'm sure you must have come across this little herb I have here; here let me rub it on your wound," said Roll Mine, magically producing a little herbal plant with its leaves in his hands.

Tommy allowed the sweet little dwarf to help him. Roll Mine had come especially for Tommy, who now wiped away his tears, much to the relief of the girls.

"It'll take some time to get better. But you mustn't stop playing, children! This life is full of ups and downs. You've got to keep going! You've simply got to!"

"You mean be like heroes and warriors?" asked Amiya, breaking her silence just then.

"Yes! Absolutely. We are little warriors, and the only way warriors get strong is by fighting! We dwarves have fought many wars for our people and protected our land against enemies from the dark worlds. Oh if only you knew of what struggles me and my brothers have shared... we never gave up. We kept going, and our wounds and worries went away with time," said the dwarf with deep wisdom, who by now had found a comfortable spot on a dead tree stump.

The children began feeling inspired.

"Come on kids, let's build this pathway. Before you know it, the sun will come shining again," he said, getting up just as quickly as he had sat down, picking up sticks and branches now from near the stream.

Roll Mine holds the branches with the spirit of a Viking or a sailor determined to conquer the mighty seas and oceans. So much strength seems to be in him, thought Tommy.

Amiya and Claire also found the inspiration they needed and realized a valuable lesson. Tommy now found the inner strength to forget himself after seeing Roll Mine and hearing his story about the dwarves fighting the dark forces! He wanted to be like them now.

"Come on Tommy!" said the three others to Tommy, who joined them now.

And on they all went with their mission of building that pathway. When it was done, it was time for Roll Mine to say goodbye.

"We'll miss you, Roll Mine. Come again, please," said Claire.

"I will! Always ready to help. Don't hesitate to call out my name when you need me. Take good care of yourselves now," said he, and in an instant, disappeared.

Laughing and giggling, the children walked back home, happier than ever before. They had learned a good lesson and got a lot done. They understood now what Serena's promise meant.

Back at Anita's—A Time to Let Go

of the Little Self

One fine day, it occurred to Anita to bring out her daughter's childhood toys for the three children she had grown so fond of— Claire, Amiya and Tommy. She brought out the toys from her attic; thankfully they were still in good condition. She then called up Claire.

"Claire, hello! Would you and your friends like to come over today? I've brought out some really old, but fun toys I thought you might enjoy playing with," she said to Claire in a sweet, motherly fashion.

"Toys! Yes! We love toys, Anita. Okay, let me call Tommy and Amiya. We'll come right away. We just got back from school," replied Claire.

Soon Claire, Tommy, and Amiya were at Anita's home for a play date, and Anita showed them the toys she had brought out—all wooden toys, some with unique mechanical features, no doubt carefully handcrafted many, many years ago when Anita's daughter was just a little girl.

"These are amazing!" said Tommy, picking up a little toy car at random.

Anita felt glad that the children were happy. Seeing that they were busy, she snuck into the kitchen quietly to add to the fun of their playdate. She was preparing fruit juice popsicles.

Amiya saw that there were all kinds of little dolls and trucks, little houses, buildings like fire stations and hospitals, little fountains, and

even railroad tracks in the toy basket. Claire and Tommy too were mesmerized by the great variety of interesting little pieces to hold and play with.

Suddenly, picking up a beautifully carved wooden painted figure of a Native American Indian girl, Amiya began to utter the name of a Navajo princess, thus naming the lovely toy that held a special fascination for her.

"Tiger Lily!" she cried out, and the other two looked at her holding the little Indian girl.

"Amiya, just a moment, let me have a look here," said Tommy, extending his hand and grabbing ahold of Tiger Lily. The moment he took it from her, Amiya tried to pull the toy back toward her.

A tussle ensued. To make things worse, Claire joined in, for every time the toy would fall out of Tommy or Amiya's hands, Claire would pick it up and start moving away with it so she could play with it first.

"Hey, give it back to me!" cried Amiya, and was almost about to break into tears, when a gnome of about half Tommy's size appeared.

Seeing the gnome appear out of nowhere in the middle of their tumult, they all backed off a few feet away from the center of their squabble, moving back as if that spot was struck by lightning, they didn't expect. After all, it was magic!

"A gnome!" whispered Tommy, catching his breath. "Again!"

"Go on, Tommy! Snatch that toy!" he squeaked, jumping up and down. "Do you know my name? No? It's Shortstitch... Go on... you can do it! Don't back down now!"

Tommy was taken aback and somewhat confused. On the one hand, he wanted to listen to the gnome, but on the other, something now stopped him.

He went ahead, however, and scrambled for the toy, seeing that it was lying on the floor, in no one's hand.

"Amiya, don't let him—just get it girl! You're the one who first got it, just go after it! Don't let him play with it!" shouted the gnome, Shortstitch, now this time to Amiya.

Amiya fought back tears another time and thought momentarily if she should scramble over to Tommy and fight for what she had picked up first. She felt a surge of energy to put up a fight.

Tommy was a tad bit surprised in the meantime.

"He was just now on my side! Now he's on her side! What a little devil!" he thought to himself.

Claire was watching this back-and-forth fight and Shortstitch's rabble rouser tactic from a distance. Something suddenly was clear to her— the gnome had appeared to cause more of that same trouble which they were already having. He was making all of them act against each other, she realized.

"Uh oh," she said to herself, "a bad gnome again! Heaven help us!"

And just as she said those words, Loopy Iris's sweet and serene voice echoed throughout the living room, and all over the house and garden—it sounded like the tinkling of bells.

"Remember little children,

Happiness comes from

Seeing others' needs as your own,

It comes from seeing others' happiness as your own,

A tiny cup can hold only a few drops of milk.

Even so, a selfish heart can hold only a few drops of happiness.

Enlarge your cup of feeling for others,

And it will contain as much happiness as you can ever drink."

Tommy, Amiya, and Claire all stopped dead in their tracks as they heard her voice resounding all around them, engulfing them, as if in a circle of pure light which could only be felt.

Silence ensued, and Shortstitch continued jumping up and down, saying, "Don't listen to her... listen to me!"

The children, deeply immersed in the thoughts which Loopy Iris shared with them invisibly, gave up their fight, and started seeing each other eye to eye—to apologize.

Ignoring Shortstitch, Tommy stood up with the wooden toy, and held it out to Amiya, saying:

"Here, I'm sorry, Amiya. I forgot you're like my little sister. Here, you can go first."

And gladly Amiya too saw the lesson she was learning. Pretty soon the children began offering to each other the little Indian girl with so much enthusiasm that Shortstitch disappeared due to the immense love and harmony that got created.

"I'm out of here!" he said and vanished.

Enjoying moments of sweetness, friendship, and love, the children decided they should go and see Loopy Iris out in the garden. She was very happy to see that they had listened to her sage counsel.

"How did you know to be with us at that time, Loopy Iris?" asked Claire, thoughtfully suddenly.

"Oh, there was a girl who said, 'Heaven help us,' and I was sent as an angel. Wasn't it you, Claire?" she asked, smilingly.

A sudden remembrance came to Claire of having said those words earlier, and she broke out into joyful laughter.

"Of course! How can I forget!" she said, dancing around now, twirling out of joy.

She then stopped and said to the fairy, "Thank you!", and all was well and happy again in the land of Snohomish.

Chapter 9:

Helping Henry, the Hurt Black

Bear of Snohomish Mountains

"What is it Teddy?!" spoke Amiya, as she felt her little magical teddy pulling on her blanket one night as she was sleeping. She woke up and sat in bed, rubbing her eyes and finding Teddy sitting on her blankets.

"Amiya, I've received a message from the Nature beings!" said Teddy, sounding a bit worried.

"What's the message, Teddy? What did they say?" replied Amiya, feeling curious.

"It's about a black bear in the mountains, Amiya. His name is Henry. He's hurt and he needs your help," replied Teddy, looking concerned about the hurt brother, even though he hadn't met him.

"Oh... he's hurt! That's sad..." replied Amiya, becoming alert now. "Don't worry, I'll tell Tommy and Claire in the morning. We'll do something to help him."

Teddy felt better after that, and thanked Amiya.

In the morning, Amiya met with Tommy and Claire and told them about Henry, the black bear. "We've got to help him!" said Tommy, who instantly wanted to bring all the possible healing to Henry.

"Yes, but how?" asked Claire. "We don't know where he is! And what are we going to heal him with?"

"Serena, the waterfall fairy will know! Come on! Anita will be happy to take us to the waterfall!" replied Tommy, and off they went to Anita's home.

At Anita's pretty little pink and green, nature-blessed home, they found their friend Anita full of sympathy, agreeing to their plan.

"Children, it's mighty nice of you to want to help a black bear, but I'm also just a little concerned. Bears can be dangerous, you see..." she said.

"Don't worry, Anita. If the Nature beings help us, we'll be fine. And Serena will protect us—she's magical, remember?" said Tommy, putting his most enthusiastic self forward, wanting to take this opportunity to practice the art of healing—something he felt called to do in life later on when he grew up.

"Hmm... you have a point—Serena has enabled you to commune with all nature and animals are a part of Nature. But promise me, children, that you will be wise. Animals need love, and sudden movements make them afraid. That's one thing to keep in mind," explained Anita.

Tommy, Amiya and Claire promised to be careful.

In a couple of hours, Anita drove them to the national park where they met Serena, the waterfall fairy, queen of all fairies and Nature beings— beauty surrounded her, all nature seemed to be singing. On this day, birds were flying around her in a sweet harmony, as though worshipping her.

What followed was a very inspiring lesson from Serena on how to care for the black bear.

Understanding the location where Henry would be found, the children started hiking till they finally saw the wounded black bear near one of the oldest trees, close to a less used walking path. He was on the ground, squirming in pain, whining a little. Every now and then he would get up and try to walk, but his left foot was hurt, and he couldn't get very far.

Anita and the children approached with calm patience.

Henry, realizing suddenly that humans were around him, started growling loudly.

"Aaarrhhh! Arrhhhhh!..."

"Anita! He's growling!" cried Claire, and instantly hugged Anita's body, for she felt scared. Tommy and Amiya backed off a little, as they realized that Henry didn't trust them.

Just then, as if to scare them away, Henry picked up a nearby broken branch and threw it in their direction.

Instantly, Anita held on to all of them and pulled them back. The children were shocked by the bear's actions, and along with Anita, they began to move backward pretty fast.

"We should stay away; he's frightened, children," said Anita, with urgency. "Come on! We should go back."

After having walked backward a bit, keeping their eyes on Henry still, who was almost out of sight now, Amiya changed her mind, and spoke up.

"Anita, wait! I think he trusts us now. We have to go back and help him," she said, her wisdom beginning to step in and understand Henry in a deeper way.

"What do you mean? You saw he's aggressive, Amiya!" said Claire.

"No, he sees we backed away when he signaled us to. So he knows we're listening to him," replied Amiya and, looking pleadingly at Anita, she asked another time. "Please Anita, we should try one more time."

Anita, very reluctantly, agreed.

Amiya started moving back in Henry's direction, but only one step at a time; this time, she spoke gently to Henry as she walked back toward him.

"I think you hear me, Henry, and I think you understand me. I'm your friend, and I want to help you, little bear," she said, as softly as possible, but with strong conviction.

After she had made considerable progress walking toward Henry step by step, she hoped that Henry would start to feel her loving intentions.

Henry, the bear, had noticed the return of Amiya. She was only a few feet away now. He could sense this time that Amiya was kind and empathetic. He hesitatingly allowed her to come close, though he was still whining with pain.

"Just let yourself be healed, Henry," said Amiya, pulling a medicinal herb from a nearby plant species that Serena had described to them. She quickly tore the leaves into little pieces, and feeling confident now that Henry was calmer, covered his wound with the herbal plant's wet leaves.

Henry let out a little growl; this time he did not do anything aggressive, however. The bear understood that he was being helped.

Feeling joyful, Amiya looked back at the others and saw that they were closer, too smiling and shining with hope; all of them felt victorious about having established a connection with Henry at last.

Once back home, Tommy got busy thinking how they could further help Henry in the coming days and weeks. Claire and Amiya also joined him in his brainstorming.

"You did the right thing, Amiya," said Anita later that evening. Amiya smiled peacefully; she felt she had learned to face her fears.

Chapter 10:

Tommy is on a Mission

Tommy woke up the next morning with a desire in his heart.

"I must find out how we can help Henry heal completely in the coming days. It must not be easy for him to walk around like that," he said to himself while getting ready for school.

All day at school he kept wondering about what he could possibly do; he felt so much love for the black bear now.

Back home after school, he called up Anita.

"Anita, I am wondering if the herbs Amiya applied on Henry's leg were enough. Maybe we should do something more to make sure he heals soon," he said to her.

Anita thoughtfully replied, "You must be right, Tommy!"

Thinking for a moment then, Tommy said, "Could we speak to Loopy Iris about some magical tricks with which we can heal Henry? She likes to teach us things."

"That sounds like a smart idea, Tommy!"

And so it was decided. Soon, Tommy, Amiya, and Claire were in Anita's garden.

The children felt delighted this day to find that instead of one fairy, two fairies were waiting for them, fluttering above their favorite fairy house. They were going to make a new friend that day.

The new fairy who had joined Loopy Iris spoke to them, "My name is Calypso, and I am the guardian fairy for our Great and Grand Silver Fir Tree here."

The children were in awe of Calypso; she had the most beautiful, colorful wings. They went ahead and introduced themselves. Tommy also spoke about his wish to help Henry, the black bear, heal further.

Calypso spoke with great wisdom now, "Children if you want to learn the secrets of life, any tricks, or methods, look within—there you will find your answers to the deepest of life's mysteries."

Silence followed. The children blinked their eyes open and closed for a moment, trying to understand Calypso.

Loopy Iris jumped in at this point. She prompted the children to sit in a relaxed way and close their eyes. The children did as they were guided. "Think now with all your heart, search for the answers deep within," murmured Calypso, herself also becoming quiet.

Moments of peace and silence, only the birds could be heard chirping; the grass felt nurturing underneath them, the sky and the breeze elevating to the spirit.

Tommy then opened his eyes and said, "Fairies, I'm feeling that the things we say can make us feel good or bad."

"That is very true, Tommy.... and?" replied Calypso.

"Well, what if we said nice things about Henry, you know, like wishing him well, wishing him all the healing and health and good things?" Tommy wondered out loud.

"That's a great idea!" said Anita, who had just walked up to them and joined them.

"When you give something to someone, how do you give it, Tommy?" asked Calypso.

"Huh? By handing it to them... with my hands!" he said, his enthusiasm skyrocketing now due to all the answers coming from within him.

"What if you raise your hands, palms facing the direction in which Henry would be, and send the positive thoughts to him by saying them out loud?" asked Calypso, hints of a smile appearing on her face, beckoning Tommy to realize more and more.

"Okay, yes, why not!" said Tommy.

"And what if we also try to imagine Henry in rainbow colors?" said Claire now.

"Why would that be?" said Anita.

"Colors make us feel better. I always feel happy when I see a rainbow," she answered.

"Oh! Wonderful!" said Anita, and the others agreed. Calypso was all smiles now.

"Children you've found your answers. Let's practice doing this," said Calypso and they all practiced the techniques they came up with together for some time.

"Now keep this practice every day!" said Calypso and sprinkled each one with a special fairy dust at the end to bring them a special kind of fairy joy.

Thanking the fairies, and Anita, the children departed and practiced their newfound techniques for a whole week. After that, they made a trip to the Wallace Waterfall. Speaking with Serena for some time, they now went looking for Henry.

Henry, to their surprise, was as good as any old black bear. He had healed completely, much to the children's joy.

"Are you seeing what I'm seeing, Claire, Amiya...?" said Tommy, eyeing Henry walking slowly toward them. He was walking normally.

"Yeah, he's fine now!" said the other two, excitedly.

Coming very close, Henry stopped and sent them a grateful little growl during which they heard his thoughts, to their great surprise.

"Thank you. I am well now."

"Did that bear just speak to us?" said Anita, filling up with pure gladness. They all broke out into joyful laughter.

"We can hear him; it must be Serena's doing," said Claire, who remembered Serena with a special fondness always.

Bidding Henry a farewell now, the children returned home happy, feeling their mission was accomplished. Peace was thus restored to the forests and beings of Snohomish county, and the children and Anita were perfectly content that Nature magic had proven to work in the toughest of times.

Chapter 11:

Growing Up

Tommy, Amiya, and Claire sat one cloudy afternoon in raincoats out in Tommy's garden, doing a little brush clearing to create a little bird's nest in a safe spot; they were hopeful that one of the colorful birds that visited Tommy's garden may just decide to make a home in that nest.

Bringing little pieces of sticks for the nest, and clearing away portions of a bush, Amiya and Tommy got to talk about the subject of 'growing up', apparently a much debated upon subject.

"When I grow up, I want to be a healer," said Tommy. "What about you, Amiya?"

"Umm... well, I don't really want to grow up. There's always so much to learn, and the adults want us to become like them," grumbled Amiya.

"Yeah, grown-ups want us to do so many things," confirmed Claire, passing to and fro with sticks. "But sometimes I like doing things; I think I want to be a singer when I grow up."

Tommy and Amiya looked at Claire for a moment, and then resumed their joint grumbling this time.

"When I'm at home, my mom is always telling me to do this or that—and then I have to do it all by myself!" said Amiya.

"And not just that—adults want us to do things just like them. Like, the other day I was setting the table and my mom corrected me again and again till I set the table exactly like her, all straight and orderly, as she would say," spoke Tommy, revealing just why he didn't like being told what to do.

"Poor you, Tommy. My dad is like that. He teaches me how to brush my teeth in exactly the way he does it. I tell him to help me do it, but then he says I have to be the one doing it," said Amiya.

A rushing sound could be heard suddenly, and the two of them turned around to see Claire having cleared away a whole pile of leaves, dropping them suddenly in a new spot. It looked like Claire was trying to get their attention.

"Aren't you both forgetting something?" piped Claire now.

"Are we?" asked Tommy, stopping his grumbling. "What are we forgetting?"

"The Nature beings, silly! They've been teaching us lessons all this while!" Claire said, sounding important for having spoken a revelation.

Amiya and Tommy had a moment of realization. Amiya turned her gaze downward now, sighing.

"Don't you think they made us grow? It's not so bad, I think," said Claire again.

"It's just not easy. I like the fairies, but the grown ups and teachers at school—they make such a fuss!" confessed Amiya.

Just then, on a wave of the incoming wind, gently drifting into sight, was the thin ethereal form of someone known to them—none other than Serena, queen of all fairies—Serena, their very own beloved waterfall fairy!

"Hello, children. You seem to be discussing something important," spoke Serena in a solemn, yet bell-like tinkling voice, reminding them of the purest things in the world.

"Serena, we were just talking about you!" said Tommy, charged with awakening, while Claire came running to join them. Amiya stood up straight now, and forgot what she was saying or doing. All of them focused their full attention on their friend.

"I came specially today to let you know that growing up is important," said Serena, gliding from side to side in the little garden. She now glided over to the bird's nest they had created and sprinkled some fairy dust into it.

"This nest you have—it's for baby birds to be born, isn't it?" she asked gently.

"Yes," replied Amiya, thinking of the tenderness of little babies.

"Wouldn't it be sad if the baby birds never learned to fly?" said Serena, the wind fluttering her transparent, ethereal, silver-white robe.

"Yes, that would be strange," replied Tommy.

Serena then went ahead and related the story of baby birds to their own lives.

"Children, you too are like these baby birds who have to learn to fly. Growing up is learning how to fly and learn all that which you came to learn in life," she went on.

Gliding closer to them, she now said a few words in parting:

"If you want to continue learning the secrets of magic from Nature beings, fairies, and other creatures, you must continue learning and growing—that means everything you're taught at school, and here at home."

"It's only when you believe in magic that you learn it. Same with growing up—when you understand that your duties are for your own good, and that they help you care for yourself, and for your loved ones, then you will naturally open yourself and enjoy growing."

"You must believe in growing up and taking responsibilities on your shoulders," said Serena, emphasizing her last words.

"Unless you do that, you won't be able to retain the power of magic either. I bid you farewell now..." she said softly and slowly glided away with the wind.

All three stood stunned, thinking deeply. One by one, seeing Serena's last glimpses fade in the distance, they began to move around and pick up little pieces of sticks which earlier they'd sectioned away—these were the big ones not suitable for the nest.

Tommy noticed then that Amiya was shivering; Claire offered Amiya her own scarf.

"I'll take care of all these sticks," said Tommy then. "Both of you can go inside and sit by the fireplace."

Appreciative of the comforting idea, Amiya and Claire went and sat inside the house, waiting for him by the fireplace, having decided by now that they wanted to grow up after all.

Tommy had decided the same thing, and shared his decision when he came in.

Later in the week, when Claire visited Anita's house, she found the little gnome, Mucklebuckle, again. He was feeling sad again and trying to shirk his duties. She got inspiration for how she would motivate him.

"Mucklebuckle, don't you think that if you do your job well a few times, the fairies will send you to the places you want to go?" she asked him.

"You think so?" he said, instantly straightening up.

"Yeah! Like, my mom and I play music for people at festivals and fairs. Maybe you'll get to do something for the fairy folk! But only if you do this job well first! I've learned that when you do your duty well, you get to go to your next step. It's like I practice my violin at home, and if I learn my songs well, I get to play for a lot of people," she clarified.

"Oh that sounds fun! Hmmm... that sounds promising. Yes, I suppose that's how it works. I do remember someone having said something like that to me once; oh, how could I have forgotten that part?!" said Mucklebuckle to himself, scratching his head.

From then on Mucklebuckle became patient and willing to do his jobs and duties well—all the places he cleaned felt happy and beautiful; his good attitude reflected in all the spaces in Anita's home.

Thus, the children learned the importance of growing up and helped their little friends also to learn to start embracing the idea of growing up.

Chapter 12:

A Friendly Visit to the Dolphins

"Children, guess where we're going this weekend?" said Amiya's mom one day as Amiya, Claire and Tommy were playing in Amiya's room.

"We're going somewhere?" asked Tommy, his interest piquing.

"It's all settled. I've spoken to your parents—we're going to Puget Sound!" she responded to their curious and eager looks.

"What's Puget Sound?" piped Claire.

"It's a vast body of water—an estuary, dear. What I mean is we're going to the beach to see dolphins!" she sparkled with a smile brimming with joy.

"Dolphins!" screamed the children with joy and started running around the room.

Amiya came and hugged her mom in the wild frenzy that ensued, thanking her mom with her tender hug.

"Oh, thanks a lot, Mumma," she cried.

"You're welcome, honey," replied her mom with a cheerful smile and a warm hug.

As the weekend approached, the excitement grew. Finally, on the day of the journey, they all piled into Amiya's family's big van. The drive was sunny and beautiful that day, and the wind not so chilly.

Arriving at the beach, Amiya, Tommy and Claire ran out before Amiya's mom could stop them and went straight to the very edge of

the waters. Amiya's mom had given them a nice talk about guidelines to follow at the beach during their car ride.

"Do you see them?" asked Tommy.

"No, I don't see them. Do you, Claire?" asked Amiya, a little crestfallen at not having them in sight.

A few people were walking around, some were swimming.

"Umm... are those the bottlenose dolphins?" said Claire, who was looking at the water a little ways away to their left.

Splashing in the water, some feet away from the shore, were what seemed like a joyful little lot of grey sea creatures, some jumping up and down in the ocean, and others just barely peeking through the water's surface.

"It's them! It must be! Come on!" shouted Tommy and went running down the beach. Claire and Amiya followed him; Amiya's mother joined them.

No sooner had they started splashing water around, while keeping an eye out for the dolphins, hoping they would come near, then the dolphins started sounding out echoes. The children stopped playing with the water, and stood watching them, patiently listening. Amiya, especially, reminded Tommy and Claire that perhaps they would be able to understand their language.

And she was right—one by one their sweet-sounding echoes turned into echoing voices, coming nearer and nearer as the dolphins decided to get closer to the shore. Holding their breaths, the children walked into the water a little more, and just as they realized they shouldn't go in any further, two dolphins came very close to them, as if they came to greet them.

"Eeeek..... eeek.... oooo.... Friendship is the song... it is the breath of life..... you can learn it too...." came their magical echoes, clear as crystal thoughts pulsating in the children's minds who were thrilled to understand their language.

The sweet dolphins let the children rub their backs and bellies.

Giggling and laughing joyfully, Tommy, Amiya, and Claire opened to new possibilities they never thought were possible.

Thoroughly enjoying themselves with the two dolphins that had come, the children soon came back toward the shore where Amiya's mother was sitting on a beach towel.

"That must have been fun!" she smiled and said.

"Yeah, that was so fun, Mumma!" replied Amiya, sitting down and reflecting a bit. "I wish I could make more friends like the dolphins. They came to us just like that! Like they knew us!"

All the way back home, the children now began talking about their amazing experiences.

"Wasn't it wonderful to play with them? They were so friendly, and they didn't even bite!" spoke Claire, feeling happy about the last part.

"I think that we can be like the dolphins, and we can make so many more friends! I loved how they just came to us!" said Amiya, enchanted.

"Yeah, so true! I learned something too—that we should share happy feelings with others," said Tommy, and everyone agreed wholeheartedly.

Soon after their return, the children began making new friends on their journey through childhood in Snohomish County. Many children joined their adventures. However, their magical ones remained a secret between the three of them.

Chapter 13:

Galad Sar's Song of Love

Early one morning in the neighborhoods of Snohomish County, close to the mountains, a haunting and soulful melody could be heard—it came from a faraway flute. The sun had not risen yet, a mist was in the air, and this beautiful song was being played by a Nature being deep in the heart of the Snohomish Mountains.

Amiya woke up suddenly from the sound of the tune. Looking up at the slightly open window, Amiya said, "I wonder if someone is sad... it feels like the song is calling someone."

Teddy, who was sitting awake nearby, replied to her words:

"I think you're quite right, Amiya—it feels like someone is remembering something, and almost as if.... hoping..."

Teddy was deep in thought as well.

"I think we may need to visit the waterfall again, Teddy!" said Amiya.

"You may be right," replied Teddy, yawning and going back to sleep.

Later in the day, Amiya met Tommy and Claire who said that they had also heard the song of the flute; it continued every now and then throughout the day. It was loud and clear every time they heard it.

Requesting Anita to take them on a hike once again to Wallace Waterfall, so that they could find out if someone needed some cheering up, they began hiking in the afternoon. Soon they came to the waterfall.

"No sign of Serena today..." said Anita, matter-of-factly, sitting down.

Just then they heard the flute song again; it was coming from the opposite bank. It was the tall and handsome elf they had seen long back; he was sitting on a rock and playing an ancient-looking flute facing the waterfall.

"He feels lost in his song," said Claire, admiring the haunting sound.

"It's a sad song, isn't it? Should we go and speak to him?" asked Amiya, thinking out loud.

"Yes, why not. You could ask him if something troubles him," replied Anita.

Amiya agreed, and along with Claire and Tommy, took the wooden walking bridge nearby to go to the opposite bank.

Coming close to the elf, they touched him gently on the shoulder.

He didn't stir and kept on playing. So, the children gave him a gentle shaking this time.

"Oh... hello little children. I didn't see you; I'm sorry if I disturbed you. Are you looking for something?" said the charming and handsome wood elf.

"What's your name, Mister?" asked Tommy.

"My name is Galad Sar, children. I sing for Serena, the fair queen fairy who lives at this heavenly abode of the waterfall. Have you met her?" he asked.

"Yes, we know Serena," replied the children. Soon Anita joined them.

"The children thought your song sounded sad," said Anita to Galad Sar, politely.

"Oh..." he said, sighing momentarily, and looking the other way to hide his face and expressions. "It is a song of love. Those are usually sad."

"Do you love someone?" asked Claire, who was aware of how older girls and boys talked.

"Yes, but you won't understand," said Galad Sar, staring now at the waterfall; the deep rushing sound that was loud and clear was comforting to hear just then.

"We'll understand; try us!" said Tommy, enthusiastically.

Galad Sar looked at them with a sad face but decided to try.

He spoke to them of a time long, long ago when Serena walked on land in the human form; that is when he first met her and fell in love at first sight. The children wondered what 'fell in love' meant. But they kept listening.

"Ever since the day Serena became protector of all lands, children, and an ever-living spirit residing here at the waterfall, I've tried to win her love and affections by singing to her love songs that spoke of two souls, meaning us both, meeting after many lifetimes," he explained.

"Serena doesn't seem touched by my heartfelt songs. I am especially sad today because of the rejection I feel from Serena. My songs are louder too, the whole valley can hear them; I nearly gave up today," he added.

"What if you sing her a happy song?" said Tommy in response to his story.

"A happy song? Well, I never thought of that... never indeed. But how can that help?" questioned Galad Sar, looking doubtful.

"Oh, it will help! All you have to do is be happy! I know it! Sing her a happy song, Galad Sar! Like the one we've learned at school. We also clap our hands and stamp our feet with the words. Claire, Amiya, sing it with me..." began Tommy and went on to sing the happy song.

"When you're happy and you know it, clap your hands....

When you're happy and you know it, stamp your feet.....

When you're happy and you know it, and you really want to show it,

When you're happy and you know it, clap your hands.

When you're happy and you know it, wiggle your ears.

When you're happy and you know it, say hello, He-LLo!"

And on and on the children sang and danced together happily for Galad Sar, who became joyful and happy for once, singing this childlike children's song. The joy was infectious, and it lightened his mood. After much coaxing from Anita, he decided to sing it to Serena. He learned the steps to the song, and the lyrics, and finally, walked over closer to where Serena usually appeared. He began performing the charming little children's song, after calling out Serena's name.

In some time, when he was done with one whole round, and Serena was still not to be seen anywhere, he began walking back to them with a sad and disappointed face. However, just then, Serena appeared.

The children shouted and yelled. Galad Sar turned around and saw that Serena had come, and with a smile on her face—finally, after ages of avoiding him, she now appeared for him.

She spoke a few words in Elvish, and out of immense joy, Galad Sar fell on his knees and spoke back to Serena in Elvish. The children were beside themselves secretly with joy.

"Maybe this is what he means by 'falling in love,'" said Amiya. "He's fallen on the ground!" Tommy, Claire, and Anita laughed at Amiya's interesting analysis and it was a happy moment for everyone.

Soon, Galad Sar came back and thanked the children.

"I never thought something so childlike and simple could draw from Serena the loving response I'd been hoping for ages and ages. Thank you! Oh thank you, children!"

Tommy, Amiya, Claire and Anita were thrilled about being able to help Galad Sar that day. After that they made their way back home and went to bed that night, dreaming dreams about loving friends and joyful songs of happiness.

Chapter 14:

A Tea Party to Understand

Responsibility

One afternoon, as Amiya, Claire, and Tommy were playing with some of Anita's daughters' toys, they discovered a picture of a little girl who looked a lot like Anita. Curious, they asked Anita about her.

"Oh, that's... my daughter. I'll tell you three about her another time," she said, trying to talk them out of the subject. But the children wanted to know more and insisted that she share.

"Okay, if you insist so much! Come over tomorrow for a special garden tea party, and I'll tell you children everything about my daughter, Melissa," she replied.

The next day, the children came over with some goodies, since they were going to have a tea party in Anita's garden.

To their surprise, the garden was decorated with tea light candles and flowers, and a lot of yummy treats were lying waiting in baskets on a big cloth near the fairy house. Anita also brought out a big teapot and little cups with trays to go with it.

Anita now began her story about Melissa.

"Melissa was a lot like you all, once upon a time," she began.

"She and I used to be very happy together in this little house. She was the apple of my eye, my shining star—my precious gem. Often, she was found playing around the garden with the fairies. Yes, with the fairies! Just like you! She loved them; she could see them. Always laughing and smiling—that was my Melissa," said Anita, reflecting on years gone by.

"But as she got older, I became somewhat of an irritable person. I used to get angry with her sometimes for not doing things the right way," said Anita.

Tommy knew that feeling, finding his mother often correcting him and losing patience sometimes in the process.

"So what happened?" asked Tommy, curious.

"Well, one day I became very angry with her for something. I lost my temper completely, and Man-doom, the little gnome who comes when someone is angry, appeared, tricking me into becoming more angry. Sadly, Melissa was deeply saddened, and moved away then, to Japan. She would have gone to college nearby if things had been good between us. But that day it all changed. She never forgave me for that day, and never returned," spoke Anita, now sounding very sad.

"We're really sorry, Anita," said Amiya, who could feel Anita's heart.

"Yes, I am too. I learned since then that love and kindness are more important than any perfection or anything. The people in our life are more important than anything else," said Anita, thinking about all she had learned.

"By being angry, we make the mistake of not being happy in our life," continued Anita.

"We need to be thankful, for everything?" asked Claire.

"Yes, Claire. That's the lesson, and most of all, we need to accept life," replied Anita.

"How I wish I could see her again, after all these years. Because she believed in magic, I believe that her life must be guided by the natural beings, there wherever she is," said Anita, cheering up a little.

"That's nice," said all three of the children together this time.

"Nature beings like fairies don't get angry, I've noticed," said Tommy.

"That is right, Tommy. And remember, it's part of learning to be responsible in life when you learn to let go of anger. It's a skill! You all can develop it," Anita said with enthusiasm.

Charged with the wisdom which Anita offered through her story, the children began talking about how to practice calmness.

Suddenly, a fairy appeared—one whom they had never seen before. She hovered playfully behind the children, trying to play hide-n-seek. The children laughed and tried to find her.

Anita got up and announced that it was about time for the children to return home since it was getting to be 6 o'clock. She walked into the house with the tea-pot then, prepared to wrap up everything.

The moment she was out of sight, the little fairy came in open view, and spoke to the children like an army general:

"Children, I am your fairy guide for the evening—my name's Everglade. We have very little time now; you must all learn to clean up after yourselves, especially after a tea party. I have orders from Serena to teach you how to go about this job today," said Everglade, the fairy, loud and clear.

Delighted by a new challenge coming their way—a new lesson from Serena—the children followed along.

They started picking up utensils one by one, and asking Everglade every now and then if they were doing things the right way. The fairy kept guiding them moment by moment, flying here, and flying there, catching things that were about to fall, giving an extra push of strength here and there, till at last, the three children had wrapped up the entire area into neat bundles to be carried into the kitchen. The grass was now clean and neat as before, and the children smiled with triumph.

"We did good!" said Tommy, standing back and admiring their hard efforts.

Anita walked out just then, and lo! She was stunned to find it all cleaned up!

"My goodness, children! Such angels! Where did you learn to take responsibility like that!" cried Anita, happily, feeling comforted by the efforts of the children to help her.

"Oh, we have some secrets," said Claire, watching Everglade wink at them from behind the fairy house, and finally disappearing out of sight.

On the way back, Amiya commented thoughtfully, "That was a lot of responsibility, wasn't it?"

"That's right, Amiya!" replied Tommy.

Thus, entrusted with wisdom, and guided with care, the children were growing up responsibly.

Chapter 15:

A Dream House in the Backyard

Garden

One morning, not long after the tea party in Anita's garden, Claire woke up with a strong feeling in her heart—it was a desire to have a little cozy home of her own, just like Anita.

At once she approached her father and appealed to him for a home of her very own.

Claire's father and mother listened in silence to her request.

"Claire, honey, when you grow up one day, you'll have an apartment all to yourself," said her mother with love and understanding.

"Oh, but I want a house now, mother," insisted Claire. "Anita's house feels so magical, and snug—she's got every possible thing stored in there, and she feels so content with it. I want to have that too!"

"A little girl with big dreams!" exclaimed her father. "Claire, sweetie, do you realize that if we get you your own house, it'll be your responsibility to take care of it, and manage it?"

Claire paused, and thought for a moment.

Finally coming to a decision, she said:

"Um, yes Daddy. I know. And I promise I'll take good care of it. I've been learning how to be responsible."

"Have you now? Good for you! Okay, then, let's get you your very own tree house. And mind you, I'll need your help in building it," exclaimed her father, sounding pleased.

Overjoyed, Claire hugged her father, who now winked at his wife and whispered to her, "Don't worry dear, it'll be kid-friendly... it's going to be safe."

Later in the week, the tree house parts arrived. By then, Claire had made the effort to extend the invitation to build it to Tommy and Amiya also, both of whom got excited and decided that if someday they were all going to build their own homes when they grew up, they might as well begin now and learn how to build a house. They agreed that it would be a learning experience.

The first day of building the tree house came. The three children were dressed head to toe in little builder clothes which their mothers had bought for them. It was going to be tough work and they were about to get dirty while sanding, shaving, cutting, drilling, and nailing pieces of wood together.

"Ready?" asked Claire's father.

"Ready!!" yelled back the children with enthusiasm.

They began their afternoon and evening shifts working on the tree house in Claire's backyard garden. The tree was selected, and measurements were taken. Math and numbers came in handy— Tommy and Claire got to practice their addition and subtraction in the process, while Amiya was content with her counting skills that she had recently learned at school.

On one of the days, Claire felt exhausted and almost gave up her responsibilities for others to do when suddenly she could sense the presence of Everglade, the silver fir guardian fairy. Ever faint, but clear like the tinkling of bells, Everglade's gentle thoughts were picked up by Claire:

"Little one, take a break, refresh yourself, but return to your tasks soon. Don't give up on this dream now that you've started. It's your responsibility."

Claire, looking around the entire 360-degree panorama around her, and not finding the fairy nearby, smiled to herself. She realized that Everglade was guiding them silently, invisibly.

Finding herself comforted, Claire found her strength after a short break, and came back to her tasks joyfully for the building of the tree house.

After a few days, when the tree house was finally ready, and even painted (painting was especially messy and fun for Tommy, Amiya and Claire), the children gathered together to see their final masterpiece from below the tree—it was amazing to behold!

"The house looks amazing! We did it!" cried Tommy.

"Can we climb up now and sit inside it?" asked Amiya thoughtfully.

"We sure can!" replied Claire, thankful that she had listened to Everglade's tinkling echoes in the wind a few days back. Her dream had come true—all because she decided she wouldn't quit and would rather act responsibly.

As the children now made a nice and cozy space out of the little tree house, complete with a little rug, tea-set, and little mock home furniture, they were visited by a little hummingbird who came hovering outside the window of their tree house.

She flapped her colorful green-grey wings at a very fast speed. And not just that—she also communicated with them:

"Hi! I am Ming from Wallace Waterfall, children. Serena sent a message for you. She says she is pleased with the three of you!"

Delight filled the air. Tommy, Amiya and Claire thanked Ming, and wanted to talk more with her, but Ming was running several errands for Serena that day and had to leave immediately.

"I have to go now. I shall see you three again, soon."

And just like that, she whizzed away.

"Ming is helping Serena... I wish I could do errands for Serena. I would fly and fly wherever I wanted!" reflected Amiya out loud. The other two agreed that it would be fun to be a hummingbird.

And thus, the children felt that they had grown older and more mature over several weeks, finding immense satisfaction in the wise choices they had made. They now had a full-fledged tree house, and they were going to spend a lot of time there together.

Chapter 16:

A Gift for Serena

"Claire? Amiya? I think we should do something for Serena," said Tommy one afternoon to Amiya and Claire as they all sat in the tree house.

"You're always wanting to do something, aren't you, Tommy?" said Claire, with a touch of wisdom.

"Umm," said Tommy, scratching his head, "yeah!"

It was funny to watch Tommy that way. The two girls looked at each other and giggled.

"Okay, what should we do?" replied Claire then.

"I don't know. Shall we ask Anita?" asked Tommy.

"Yes!" said Amiya.

And so, off they went to their best neighborhood friend who was more dear to them than any friend they had ever had.

Arriving at Anita's, the children sat down and explained Tommy's idea.

"That is a wonderful idea, children! How very thoughtful of you, Tommy!" said Anita, bringing them some lemon tea and little salty treats to eat with it.

"But we don't know what we should do for her," said Claire.

Anita kept silent for a moment while she thought things through and served them.

"You know what, children? Serena is a fairy, and not a human being with a house or things in it. Serena is everywhere in a sense as she is Queen of all Nature beings. She doesn't need anything from anyone, if you think about it," she began, and the children momentarily began to droop and sigh and feel sad.

But Anita continued, "There is one thing, however, that everyone in this world wants, and even Serena would want it."

Listening to these words, their energy shot up their spines, and they sat up straight, hanging on Anita's every word. Tommy patiently asked, "What's that, Anita?!"

"I'll put it like a riddle; see if you can figure it out," replied Anita mischievously.

Smiling, the children agreed.

"It's invisible.... can't be touched with hands.... and it fills you up when you get even a little bit of it... guess what it is," said Anita.

Tommy, Amiya, and Claire looked around and ran through their little brains, trying to think what that thing could be.

Suddenly, words from Tommy erupted like a volcano.

"LOVE!" he shouted out, almost falling from his place on the couch in his enthusiasm.

Smiling proudly, Anita replied, "You've got it, Tommy!"

And the girls smiled and repeated to themselves, "Love, love.... hmmm... love!" Shuffling around on the couch, they wondered though. They looked at Tommy who repeated the word to them. Tommy went on to explain in his own 8-year old's wisdom how that was the answer by giving examples from his life.

"Okay, so can we give love to Serena?" asked Claire, feeling sure of the answer herself now. "And if so, how do we do it Anita?"

Anita picked up a cookie and began to munch on it.

"Love," she said, after eating a bit, "is a feeling, a vibration which you can fill things with. Take anything and you can fill it with the invisible love in your heart. It's possible."

"Oooh!" said the children, wonderstruck.

"Anything at all; Water, a leaf, a flower, a pen, a stone, a drawing—anything you want!" continued Anita.

"Calypso once taught me how to do this—just keep the thing in front of you, let's say a leaf or a flower, surround it with your hands, giving some space between your hands and the object, like when you send healing, Tommy, and feel the invisible love flowing from your heart to the hands and then to the object, keeping in mind the person you are doing it for," explained Anita.

"Ok, but I think we could imagine love like a light, couldn't we, Anita?" said Amiya, who felt this to be true, but wanted to make sure.

"Yes, dear. That would help. Good thinking, Amiya. The point is to feel as much love as you can with your heart, which is inside you," said Anita.

And so it was decided; they were all going to find something or other that appealed to them and fill it with their love for Serena. Then they would offer it to Serena as a gift and a symbol of their thanks to her. This would be their way of saying:

"Thank you for all you've done for us, Serena!"

Chapter 17:

A Wish Fulfilled

The weekend took Amiya, Tommy, Claire and Anita to their favorite haunt— the Wallace Waterfall. Each of the children had packed their little rucksacks with their chosen items, gifts filled with love for Serena.

As soon as they approached the waterfall, they saw that Serena was singing a sweet and angelic song on her instrument; its soothing sound could barely be heard over the rushing of the waterfall, but it was heavenly.

Opening their rucksacks, the children picked up their little gifts, and stood there, with eyes closed, filling their little gifts again—with Love!

Amiya had a flower; Claire had a little pebble; and Tommy had a little something he had made out of play dough.

Soon the gifts were placed near where Serena was singing.

"What is this children?!" Serena stopped singing and exclaimed with joy the moment she realized she had company.

"They're gifts for you, Serena!" said Amiya.

"Aah, I feel your love, children; this is so sweet—thank you Amiya, Tommy, Claire," said Serena.

"And this is from me," said Anita, putting down a little rose for Serena, filled with her love.

"Thank you, I am so touched," replied Serena as she gently glided over the little gifts which they all had placed on the rocks; twirling about with joy now, and shining suddenly with sparkling light, Serena became much brighter to behold, her form more visible now.

"Wow!" gasped the children.

At once, there came a hush over the waterfall, as though the sounds became stilled. Serena's magic was felt in the air, and now a deep stillness filled the place.

Hovering at one point now, Serena said calmly, "Children, you have learned your lessons so well; you realize that gratitude is the right attitude to have toward those who teach and guide you."

"And Anita here has taught you this precious principle," she continued. "Hence, I will grant Anita a wish come true—her daughter will return to her to see her again."

And saying that, Serena waved her hand—wind blew, and clouds began to gather above them.

"That would mean everything to me, Serena. Thank you!" said Anita softly.

The children became very excited now; they could not contain their joy at that moment. "Anita will see her daughter again. Serena, you can do that?" they asked, inquisitively, also looking at each other, their expressions filled with wonder at the amazing reality of the natural world.

"Yes, and now you can wish for something for yourselves; you three deserve blessings," said Serena. "You've worked hard on yourselves."

Amiya was ready with her request as soon as Serena invited them to wish.

"Um.. Serena, I'm ready. My Barbie doll at home has a broken arm; I don't know how to fix it, and at night when the toys come alive, she feels pain. Could you heal her ouchie please?" she asked, bravely.

"Yes, indeed, Amiya," Serena replied.

At once Serena waved her hand, and shining light erupted in waves, which then disappeared as if taken on wings by the wind.

"It is done, Amiya," said Serena smilingly. "You have such a pure heart."

Claire and Tommy were next. Tommy began to name a few possible wishes. Claire joined in, thinking about the rare opportunity they got to ask for something.

"I've been wanting a PlayStation," said Tommy, "But then there's this really cool thing I saw once in a store which my parents didn't allow me to get... and I've always wanted a bicycle with seven gears..."

Claire joined in: "Serena, I want the prettiest dress that's for princesses, and my friend at school keeps saying I should get money from home so we can buy food at school. Can you make that possible? And there's a magical unicorn I've always wanted with rainbow hair and wings—I really want that!"

Serena kept listening with an even-minded calmness. She said, "Anything else, children? You can keep thinking of as many things as you want."

Tommy and Amiya, enthused that they could ask for even more than what they'd already asked, started making their wildest wishes known, things that always seemed out of reach, or they were too young for. On and on they went with their long list, till suddenly, Anita cleared her throat.

Realizing all the time that had gone by, the children stopped their listing of things all of a sudden, and a quiet silence fell on everyone.

Finally, Tommy dropped his gaze down to the ground, feeling a bit embarrassed.

"Serena, I think I don't want any of those things; I'm happier when I wish for something that makes someone else happy," he said, then looked up to find Serena with a most blissful smile looking back at him.

Claire too realized something similar.

"Serena, it's greedy of me also to ask so many things for myself. Can I ask for something for my sister?" she inquired, becoming aware of her larger reality.

"Yes, of course, you can," said Serena.

And then, both Claire and Tommy ended up asking for special blessings for their brothers and sisters.

That evening, the children and Anita went back home with the happiest and truest of feelings in her heart—feelings of a love that was pure and not selfish. They learned important lessons and awaited the fulfillment of their special prayers upon their arrival back home.

Chapter 18:

Celebrating Service

It was a beautiful Sunday morning when Claire was sitting in the tree house in her backyard garden, listening for the sound of a particular bird who had nestled on a nearby branch.

Out of the blue, suddenly, came the sound of an ice cream van, ringing a bell as it entered the front street.

"The ice cream van!" Claire said out loud.

Making her way quickly to the front door, Claire was able to draw the attention of the ice cream man who was passing out yummy flavors of ice cream to the neighborhood children.

Soon after, Claire began thinking about a community fair that was going to be held in the grounds of Snohomish County.

"Claire, honey, do you feel ready to perform 'O Come, Little Children' on your violin for the town fair? And the variation on Twinkle Twinkle Little Star?" asked her mother the day before.

"Yes, I think so, Mom," Claire had answered. Performing for the crowds that were going to come felt like a big deal to Claire. But she wanted to do more.

On the day of the visit by the ice cream man, Claire decided to share the thought of doing something more with her best friends who were also going to attend the fair. The colorful ice cream van with its many wonders just waiting to be explored put the excitement in her to offer something fun and thrilling like that to the guests who would come to the town fair.

"Tommy, Amiya, what do you think about a stall at the fair?" she asked her two best friends that day.

Tommy understood instantly that that was going to be a great way to serve others.

"Let's talk about it with Anita," said Tommy, and off they went to see Anita.

When she heard the idea, she said, "Children, it's a great idea. But you know it's going to take a lot of effort and one very important quality which you've learned—taking responsibility. You'll be handling money! And most likely you'll need a team to help you if you're going to have two or three services all at the same table," answered Anita.

"We're ready for it!" said Tommy, feeling more and more confident, and now happy that Claire thought of it.

Just then, a pretty young lady walked in from one of the rooms, wearing a blue dress, and a warm smile.

"Children, meet my daughter, Melissa," said Anita, proudly. Melissa was a sight of happiness to behold.

"Hello, my mother has told me so much about you!" said Melissa to the children.

The children and Melissa had a good time getting to know each other. In fact, Melissa offered to help them during the town fair. Claire's mind was taking her back to the meeting with Serena all that while and the magic and love that brought about the miracle of Melissa and Anita reuniting after so many years.

"I'm happy to be back here with my mom," said Melissa, sounding like a child who had learned some important lessons herself.

The day of the fair came, and the children and Melissa, along with two other friends from their neighborhood, put up a big stall with the most interesting of games, snacks to purchase and eat, and gifts for guests as part of a lucky draw that they had created for supporting a local bee-keeper. Realizing the importance of supporting the life of their local bees for Nature's preservation, the children decided to support him with the money they would make at the fair.

After playing her two songs for a big audience, Claire left the stage for her mother to perform. She then joined Tommy, Amiya and the others at their little junction where elders, youth, parents, grandparents and new people all came to enjoy freshly made lemonade which Amiya and her mother had prepared. The guests tried solving the mystery corner puzzle which Melissa had created with Tommy, who had picked up important facts from mystery stories and added real-life artistic skills of cutting and assembling to bring to life a mystery corner sectioned off from the main table. Guests also purchased tickets for the lucky draw which promised fun little things which the children and their friends had created from articles in nature.

Everything drew so much attention that soon the mayor, Mr. Jones, announced how wonderfully Claire's team had done out of all the stalls; he appreciated them all for the services and fun they had brought to the residents and guests that day, and not to forget, their efforts to support a local beekeeper.

By evening when everyone was packing up, Ming, the little hummingbird from Wallace Waterfall, flew by, quickly delivering a message to Tommy, Amiya, and Claire that Serena sent her magical blessings to them for the services they had performed on the occasion.

As soon as she said it, a wave of joy engulfed the children.

"Do you feel it?" whispered Amiya to the other two. "I'm feeling so light suddenly as if I'm going to fly."

"I feel it; it's amazing, isn't it?" said Claire.

"We're not flying! But it's just like flying!" said Tommy with a happy and peaceful feeling.

Thus ended another very meaningful adventure for Tommy, Amiya and Claire, celebrating the power of service to others.

Chapter 19:

Kindness is a Gift That Turns into

Gold

One Friday morning, as Tommy was getting ready to go to school—a day when he woke earlier than usual—a soft knock on the front door caught his attention. He went down to open the door as he knew that his mom was busy making breakfast in the kitchen.

Opening the door, with one sock on and one sock in his hand, he found a young boy, about Amiya's age, standing there in what looked like rags and torn clothes. The little boy looked slightly cold as well. His innocent eyes had joy in them, however. He seemed to be looking for something.

"Hi," said Tommy, feeling really bad for the boy and his condition, concerned for him now. "Who are you? Do you need something?"

The young boy looked around Tommy, to the left of him, and to the right, peering at whatever the open door could show him. Interest sparked in his sweet eyes.

"Do you have a toy? I don't have any toys. My home used to be nearby, but now we live in the forest. I don't have anything to play with," he said, mentioning the bare and simple facts of his life.

Tommy's heart just melted further and further and began to feel so sorry for the poor boy. He saw how unfortunate this little boy was, and at the same time, how hopeful he was of enjoying something nice. At that moment, Tommy wanted to give him everything he had.

Running up the stairs to his room, a tear ran down his face. Wishing with all his heart that the boy would attract good fortune from now on, Tommy picked up his favorite and most fancy toy, and brought it down to him.

"Here, take this. It's all yours. Do you want to come in and eat something?" he asked the boy in rags, handing over his most prized possession. He knew his mother would be fine with it.

Instantly, as if by some divine Nature magic, the little boy with sweet and innocent eyes and raggedy clothes transformed into a wise-looking, elder Navajo medicine man, a colorful shawl wrapped around his shoulders, a pretty feather sticking out from the headband he wore, a glad and grateful smile on his lips, his whole being charged with the spirit of worship, prayer, wisdom, and knowledge. He was carrying a book.

"Little boy, thank you. You have passed the test of our lady, Serena, again," he said, winking at Tommy.

Overwhelmed with reverence for magic, and the utter beauty of how things happen, Tommy could say no more than a simple "Okay..." with his mouth wide open.

"I am the medicine man who once lived here long ago when my people dwelled in these lands. Since childhood, I was trained to be a healer for my people. This book here was compiled specially for you, Tommy. It has the names of healing herbs and where they are found in this world. Your desire to be a healing hand in this world was heard, little one— this book will guide you!" he told Tommy and handed over the book with a slight bow of respect.

"Th-Thank you, Sir. How nice of you. A book for me!" he said, taking the book in his hands, feeling like it was a precious treasure box.

"You want to heal others, am I right?" said the Navajo Indian, emphatically.

Full of eagerness, Tommy filled up with an exuberance inside which was still somewhat shy to come out.

"Yes, I do, Sir," he managed to get out. Then, coming to realize that the experience was definitely real, Tommy ventured to say a few more words.

"Can people come to believe in magic, Sir?" he asked politely.

"That is a question which depends on person to person, Tommy. Everyone is different. Some have the capacity to believe in it and they do; others don't want to believe it, and they don't. And some, with a few signs, come to believe in it. Does that answer your question?" said the wise Navajo.

"I see," said Tommy, understanding the fine differences between people. "Yes, that answers."

"Farewell then, and oh wait, I almost forgot. Your Navajo name, should you ever like one, was deemed by some of us to be 'Lion Amaranth'. Hope you will like it. We shall meet again someday," he said and vanished into thin air as if he had never been there.

Dazed by the experience, Tommy now held firmly to the book in his hands, ready to dive into the wealthy treasure that would aid him in healing others when he grew up, perhaps even before that. As these thoughts passed through Tommy's head, he felt as if he could glimpse his future—a well-known healer, traveling far in foreign lands, bringing hope and healing to a world that wanted the body to heal, but more than that, a world that wanted its inner heart and spirit to heal.

Chapter 20:

A Life Journey with Nature Beings

Amiya, Tommy, Claire—all three met in the tree house on this day. It was a brilliant morning, a Sunday. The sky was bright and clear, the clouds were few and passed by with the gentle wind. Birds were chirping everywhere. The children decided it was time for an important meeting.

Climbing up the wooden steps, they huddled together in Claire's little treehouse, along with packets full of carrots and cheese sticks and some fresh juice which their moms had prepared for them to enjoy.

"So what's the meeting about, Tommy?" asked Amiya.

"The plan is this—we come up with a plan," replied Tommy, who had also carried his healer's handbook with him.

"We need a plan?" asked Claire.

"Yeah, we do! It's about our future. I want to be a healer when I grow up, I'm sure. But what about you two? What's your plan? And think about how you're going to do it," said Tommy.

"I want to be a teacher," replied Claire. "A teacher who teaches children how to sing."

"Why do you want to be a teacher?" asked Amiya, still wondering.

"Because when someone sings, they're being happy. And they learn much faster the things they should do in their life," replied Claire from her own 6-year-old's experience.

"Oh, I see," replied Amiya.

"What about you, Amiya? What do you want to be when you grow up?" asked Tommy.

"Hmmm..... I don't know. I think I'll be helping people by listening to them. When I listen to others, it's always comforting for them. And like when I am patient and just there for them, they feel loved and calm," said Amiya, speaking from her depths.

"Hm, so that would make you a guide," replied Tommy, who had heard of the word and concept.

"A guide? So that's what it's called!" sighed Amiya, looking away into the distance, also wondering of other things.

"Okay, the next part we have to decide is how we're going to become what we want to become!" said Tommy, looking at the other two.

"I know!" spurted Claire. "We can request the fairies to teach us!"

"The fairies know us now. They've taught us so many things. If we stop asking, they might go away," said Amiya, thoughtfully.

"No, we shouldn't let that happen. We should definitely keep asking them how to do things; nobody gets a chance like this to learn important things from them. We three got a rare chance! We have to keep it going!" said Tommy.

"I agree, Tommy," said Claire. "You're right."

"One day, we'll all grow up and go to different places," said Amiya suddenly, still looking out the window.

A silence came over them all—everything felt hushed for a moment. Even the birds seemed quiet. And then, Claire spoke.

"We've got to be of help to Anita, however, you two! She'll need us more as time goes on," she said, and the other two got an alert look in their eyes, their heads nodding, as if realizing what an important role Nature had given them.

"We're going to take care of her," said Amiya, almost in a whisper, though sounding strong and sure.

A strong gush of wind came out of the blue just then, shaking the branches around them. The leaves went rustling for the next few minutes, while the air became fresh as though Wallace Waterfall were nearby. The sun hid behind the clouds, and a slight coolness came about in the air.

"Good children, you make me so proud," came Serena's angelic voice from all around them.

Amiya, Tommy and Claire gasped with delight, excitedly looking about, trying to see if they could spot Serena somewhere on the grounds. But she was nowhere to be seen. She was everywhere.

Such was Tommy, Amiya, and Claire's faith in their dreams to become noble helpers one day and Serena's blessings never left them. They always had their magical friends around them throughout life. And not to forget, their best friend Anita, who continued to teach good things to them. They never forgot her, and always made a special place in their lives for Anita. Anita had their love, care, friendship, and support throughout her years on Earth.

THE END

Author Bio

Hi, I'm Bruce Henry, the author of the book. I'm from Louisiana; I'm married, have two kids and five great-grandchildren. I've put together these 20 short stories for children ages 4 to 8 years old so that little ones can relax as they go to sleep and enjoy the beauty of a peaceful and magical imagination as they doze off. The stories calm the mind with helpful thoughts at night; parents and guardians can read these rare and magical stories to the children that instill values and are pure fun to listen to! Children's happiness is dear to my heart, and I hope this book will bring calmness and joy to children everywhere.

Made in the USA
Middletown, DE
09 November 2024

64186502R00056